For Hester, who loves snails
– C.R. and A.S.

First published 2020 by Nosy Crow Ltd
The Crow's Nest, 14 Baden Place, Crosby Row
London SE1 1YW
www.nosycrow.com

ISBN 978 1 78800 830 3

Nosy Crow and associated logos are trademarks and/or registered
trademarks of Nosy Crow Ltd
Text © Camilla Reid 2020
Illustrations © Axel Scheffler 2020

The right of Axel Scheffler to be identified as the illustrator
of this work has been asserted.

A CIP catalogue record for this book is available from the British Library.

Printed in China

1 3 5 7 9 10 8 6 4 2

Pip and Posy
The Friendly Snail

Axel Scheffler

nosy crow

It was a lovely day.
Pip was doing some gardening.

Posy was having fun.

"BANG! BANG!" went her drum.
"LAAA! LAAAA!" she sang.

"BOING! BOING!" she bounced.

"Could you be a bit quieter,
please, Posy?" said Pip.

Just then, Pip found a snail.
It was very friendly.

"WHEEE!"
said Posy.

"Shhhh, Posy," said Pip.

Pip gave the snail some lettuce to eat.
The snail looked happy.

Posy appeared.
"BRRM! BRRM! BRRM!" she shouted.

The snail disappeared inside its shell.

"Posy!" said Pip. "You've scared my snail! Your games are too noisy! Go away!"

Posy felt sad.
She hadn't meant to scare the snail.

Poor Posy!

Pip raked
the earth.

He planted
some seeds.

And he sprinkled the seeds
with his watering can.

Pip didn't notice a bird looking at the snail.

The bird got closer. And closer.

And closer!

Oh, dear!

"RRRRRRAAAAAA!" roared a voice.
Pip jumped.

"GO AWAY, YOU BIG, GREEDY BIRD!"
shouted the voice again.

The bird flew
into the sky . . .

and the snail
dropped to the
ground.

Posy came out from behind the bush.

"Oh, Posy,"
said Pip.
"It was YOU!
Your loud voice
saved the snail!"

"I'm sorry, Posy," said Pip.
"Sometimes it's really good to be noisy.

Can we be friends again?"

"Yes, of course we can!" said Posy.

After that, they played a very NOISY game.

"WHOO-HOO!" shouted Posy.

"YEE-HAA!" shouted Pip.

And then they had a nice
quiet time in the garden.

Hooray!